Wish Fish

Level 2A

Written by Sam Hay
Illustrated by Katie May

Ticktock

What is synthetic phonics?

Synthetic phonics teaches children to recognise the sounds of letters and to blend 'synthesise' them together to make whole words.

Understanding sound/letter relationships gives children the confidence and ability to read unfamiliar words, without having to rely on memory or guesswork; this helps them progress towards independent reading.

Did you know? Spoken English uses more than 40 speech sounds. Each sound is called a *phoneme*. Some phonemes relate to a single letter (d-o-g) and others to combinations of letters (sh-ar-p). When a phoneme is written down it is called a *grapheme*. Teaching these sounds, matching them to their written form and sounding out words for reading is the basis of synthetic phonics.

Consultant

I love reading phonics has been created in consultation
with language expert Abigail Steel. She has a
background in teaching and teacher training and is
a respected expert in the field of Synthetic Phonics.
Abigail Steel is a regular contributor to educational
publications. Her international education consultancy
supports parents and teachers in the promotion of
literacy skills.

Reading tips

 This book focuses on the sh sound as in shop.

Tricky words in this book

Any words in bold may have unusual spellings or are new and have not yet been introduced.

Tricky words in this book:

she said I of my
was the push we

Extra ways to have fun with this book

After the reader has finished the story, ask them questions about what they have just read:

What does Meg find in the pond?
Why does Meg wish that she doesn't have a wish fish?

Explain that the two letters 'sh' make one sound. Think of other words that use the 'sh' sound, such as *ship* or *shop*.

I love reading.
I have lots of books
but I always wish
for more!

A pronunciation guide

This grid highlights the sounds used in the story and offers a guide on how to say them.

s as in sat	a as in ant	t as in tin	p as in pig	i as in ink
n as in net	c as in cat	e as in egg	h as in hen	r as in rat
m as in mug	d as in dog	g as in get	o as in ox	u as in up
l as in log	f as in fan	b as in bag	j as in jug	v as in van
w as in wet	z as in zip	y as in yet	k as in kit	qu as in quick
x as in box	ff as in off	ll as in ball	ss as in kiss	zz as in buzz
ck as in duck	pp as in puppy	nn as in bunny	rr as in arrow	gg as in egg
dd as in daddy	bb as in chubby	tt as in attic	sh as in shop	ch as in chip

Be careful not to add an 'uh' sound to 's', 't', 'p', 'c', 'h', 'r', 'm', 'd', 'g', 'l', 'f' and 'b'. For example, say 'fff' not 'fuh' and 'sss' not 'suh'.

Meg was at a pond. **She** had
a net.

Pip had got a ship.

'A fish!' **said** Meg.
'**I** am a wish fish,' it said.

Gosh!' said Meg.

'I wish I had a lot **of** cash,' said Meg.

Pop! Meg got a shock.
'A sack of cash!' she said.

'I wish **my** ship **was** big,'
said Pip.

Pop! **The** ship was big.
But it had a bad fox on it.

'I spot cash,' said Fox.
Fox got off the ship.

'Stop him!' said Meg.
'Fox will rob us!'

Pip was quick. **Push**!

Fox was wet. Fox was mad!

'Quick!' said Pip. 'A wish!'

'I wish I had not got a wish fish,' said Meg.

Pop! The wish fish, cash and Fox
vanish. The ship is not big.

Meg is sad. '**We** can get a pet fish
and a big ship at a shop,' says Pip

'Yes. But not a fox!' says Meg.

OVER **48** TITLES IN SIX LEVELS

Abigail Steel recommends...

Some titles from Level 1

Bad Rat

978-1-84898-600-8

The Best Gift

978-1-84898-603-9

Clint and Grant Play I-Spy

978-1-78325-098-1

Gran and Bret's Trip

978-1-78325-100-1

Other titles to enjoy from Level 2

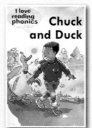

Chuck and Duck

978-1-84898-605-3

Let's go to the Swings

978-1-78325-102-5

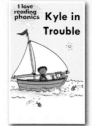

Kyle in Trouble

978-1-78325-101-8

Some titles from Level 3

Bart's Go-Cart

978-1-78325-105-6

Queen Ella's Feet

978-1-84898-609-1

Puff Flies

978-1-84898-610-7

The Pop Duel

978-1-78325-108-7

An Hachette UK Company
www.hachette.co.uk

Copyright © Octopus Publishing Group Ltd 2012
First published in Great Britain in 2012 by TickTock, an imprint of Octopus Publishing Group Ltd,
Endeavour House, 189 Shaftesbury Avenue, London WC2H 8JY.
www.octopusbooks.co.uk
www.ticktockbooks.co.uk

ISBN 978 1 84898 604 6

Printed and bound in China
10 9 8 7 6 5 4 3